AFTERSHOCK

AFTERSHOCK

GABRIELLE PRENDERGAST

ORCA BOOK PUBLISHERS

Published in Canada and the United States
in 2023 by Orca Book Publishers.
orcabook.com

Library and Archives Canada Cataloguing in Publication
Title: Aftershock / Gabrielle Prendergast.
Names: Prendergast, Gabrielle, author.
Series: Orca anchor.
Description: Series statement: Orca anchor
Identifiers: Canadiana (print) 20220453446 | Canadiana (ebook) 20220453454 |
ISBN 9781459837201 (softcover) | ISBN 9781459837218 (PDF) |
ISBN 9781459837225 (EPUB)
Subjects: LCGFT: Novels. | LCGFT: High interest-low vocabulary books.
Classification: LCC PS8631.R448 A69 2023 | DDC jC813/.6—dc23

Library of Congress Control Number: 2022948359

Summary: In this high-interest accessible novel for teen readers,
Amy and her estranged half sister, Mara, journey through
the aftermath of a massive earthquake in search of their parents.

Orca Book Publishers is committed to reducing the consumption of
nonrenewable resources in the production of our books. We make
every effort to use materials that support a sustainable future.

Orca Book Publishers gratefully acknowledges the support
for its publishing programs provided by the following agencies:
the Government of Canada, the Canada Council for the Arts and
the Province of British Columbia through the BC Arts Council
and the Book Publishing Tax Credit.

Design by Ella Collier
Edited by Doeun Rivendell
Cover photography by Getty Images/Sol de Zuasnabar Brebbia
Author photo by Erika Forest

Printed and bound in Canada.

26 25 24 23 • 1 2 3 4

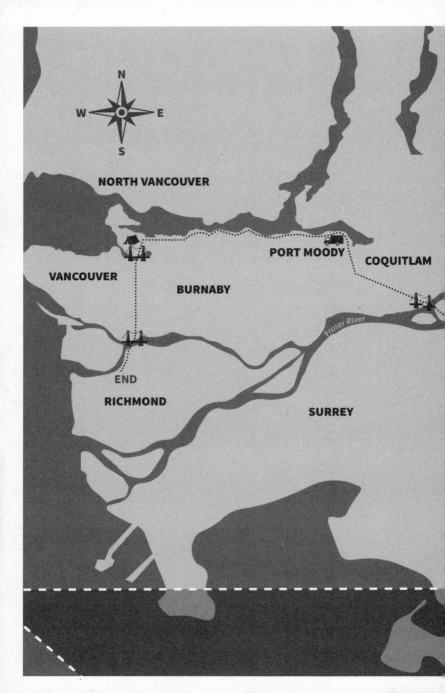

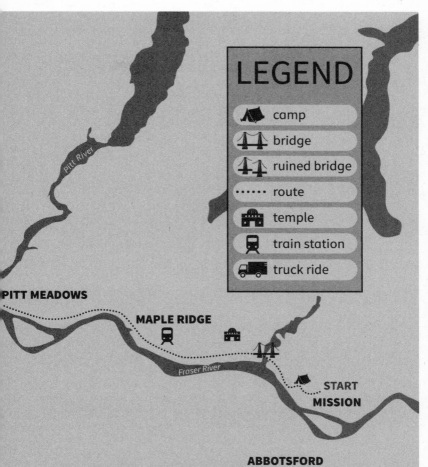

LEGEND

- 🏕 camp
- 🌉 bridge
- 🌉 ruined bridge
- ••••• route
- 🏛 temple
- 🚉 train station
- 🚚 truck ride

PITT MEADOWS

MAPLE RIDGE 🚉 🏛

Pitt River

Fraser River

🏕 START
MISSION

ABBOTSFORD

CANADA

USA

Chapter One

Finally! It's the last day of school. I'm happy. Summer is going to be great. I made some new friends this year, and we're going to hang out. Go on hikes. Maybe go to the beach. I want to try to earn some money.

I'm in tenth grade. I mean, I'm nearly *done* tenth grade. I don't hate school, but I don't love it either. I go to a private school that's not very big. Only about 300 kids go here. Our class sizes are small, so that's good. There are a lot of rules. That's not so good. But they're not too hard to follow, I guess. And we don't wear uniforms. That's good too.

The school is far away from everything. That's bad. We can't go get junk food at lunch. We can't walk anywhere. Some days Dad drives me to school. Other days I have to take the school bus. That's also bad. But it's only on the days Dad works in the city. When he needs to leave really early. Like today. That's about half the time.

I go to a K–12 school. That means we have kids from kindergarten to twelfth grade. Sometimes that's annoying. The little kids can be brats. But they can be cute too.

Right now I can hear them in the music room. It's in a separate building. Probably so the noise won't bother the rest of the school. The little kids are playing drums. Badly! It's funny though.

My friends Sofie and Peter and I are clearing up the kids' playground. We have to make sure everything is put away for summer. The little kids left balls and skipping ropes and Hula-Hoops everywhere. We also find someone's hoodie. And a mitten hidden in a bush. It must have been there since winter.

Now it's an hour until summer break starts. I can't wait. I'm excited to be done with school for a while. I'm also excited because my mom comes home from

Japan tomorrow. She's been there for nearly a month on a business trip. She's a computer programmer.

It's okay just having my dad at home. But I miss my mom. I can't wait to show her my report card. School isn't easy for me, and I worked so hard this year. It paid off. I improved my grades a lot. I think Mom and Dad will be really proud. I'm proud of myself too.

It's just the three of us at home. Me and Mom and Dad. I have a half sister, who has a different mom. But I barely know them. My half sister's name is Mara. She's two years older than me. Seventeen. Dad was married to her mom when he met my mom. It's pretty messy. We don't talk about it much. I know

Dad pays child support for her. And he sees her sometimes. But...yeah. It's messy.

Mara goes to the public high school in Abbotsford. She and her mom live near there. That's not very far from us. We live just over the river in Mission. About a five-minute drive from my school.

Dad calls it a "suburb." But really it's just a small town.

I'd like to get to know Mara better. I've only met her a few times. Once I sent her a message on Instagram, but she never replied. So that was that.

Families can be a lot sometimes.

"Amy!" Sofie calls out to me. "Did you find the other mitten?"

She and Peter walk toward the school. Peter has three Hula-Hoops around his neck. Somewhere, someone's dog starts barking.

"No!" I yell back. "But I found a pair of head-phones!" Another dog barks, like it's mad at me for yelling.

I tug the headphones out of the weeds. Suddenly the ground starts to shake! Sofie and Peter look back at me. Their eyes are wide.

Earthquake!

I expect it to be just a gentle rumble and only last a few seconds. That's happened before. But the rumbling and shaking gets worse. And it doesn't stop. Soon it's like the ground is turning sideways.

"Get away from the school!" I yell. We've all done the earthquake drills. Every kid in this part of the world has. You're supposed to get under your desk.

That's if you're inside. It's different when you're outside. You're supposed to get away from anything that can fall on you. Away from buildings or power lines. I run out into the field.

Sofie and Peter drop all the stuff they gathered. They run toward me. The ground is shaking so much I can hardly stand. Sofie and Peter can barely run. Sofie falls, and Peter drags her along.

They finally get to me. We hold on to each other. We look back at the school. The noise is incredible. Like the world is cracking into pieces. The air fills with dust.

Sofie gasps and Peter makes a noise. I hold my breath. I can't believe what I see.

The roof of the music room starts to cave in!

Chapter Two

At last the ground stops shaking.

Sofie and Peter and I stand there. We're in shock. I can't speak. Or move. My mouth is dry and my heart is pounding. My ears are ringing. No, wait. That's a siren somewhere.

A light wind starts to blow the dust away. But nothing can blow away what happened. Almost all of the windows in the school are broken. Shattered. A light pole in the street has fallen over. It landed on a car. The windshield is smashed. A garage across the street has crumpled. And car alarms are going off.

Slowly I feel my body come back. It's like waking up from a nightmare.

"Are you okay?" I ask Sofie and Peter.

Peter mumbles something. Sofie starts to run.

"The music room!" she yells.

We run after her. Kids and teachers start streaming out of the school. Lots of them are crying. They're dusty. The teachers and the bigger kids carry some of the little kids.

The gym teacher, Miss Carter, and the principal, Mr. Li, run toward the music room.

"Help me get this door open!" Sofie says. She tugs on the door. Part of the doorframe is bent. A beam from the roof landed on it.

"Be careful!" Miss Carter says.

"Step back!" Mr. Li says. He pulls on the door. But it won't budge.

I can hear some kids crying inside the music room. "They're alive!" I say. I can't believe this is happening.

Peter, Sofie and I run around the side of the music room. We can see through the broken windows. The little kids are all under the tables. Miss Singh, the music teacher, is under her desk. She's holding two kids against her.

The ceiling and part of the roof are crumbled all over their tabletops. But the earthquake drills worked. Everyone seems okay! So far.

Peter takes off his hoodie. He covers his hand with it. Then he breaks the rest of the glass from one of the windows.

"Get them out through here!" he says.

Mr. Li and Miss Carter join us. Miss Carter climbs through the broken window. She lifts the kids up. Peter, Sofie and I take them, and Mr. Li leads them out into the field. Finally Miss Carter helps Miss Singh, who is hurt. Her head is cut and she's limping.

Everyone else is out of the school. There are some injuries. But I don't think anyone died. We all line up in our homeroom groups to be counted. Just like in the drills.

Those drills. I keep thinking about them. Thank God we did them.

I sit with Sofie and Peter. Some of our class-mates sit with us. But nobody talks. We're all too shocked.

This morning all the food from the cafeteria was loaded into a truck. The school was going to donate it. The truck hasn't left yet, so at least we have some food. We're not allowed to go back into the school. It's not safe. But all our stuff is still in there. So much for my great report card.

We all try to call our parents on our cell phones. A couple of kids get through. Most don't.

I don't.

Everyone gets a bottle of water and a fruit bar. I can't eat. I sip the water. Time seems to move fast. It feels like the earthquake was weeks ago. But it's only been a few hours now.

Parents keep arriving. Sofie's dad runs from his car.

"Sofie!" he yells. Sofie cries as they hug.

Both of Peter's moms turn up. They put their arms around him.

"Do you want to come home with us?" one of Peter's moms asks.

"No, I'll wait for my dad," I say.

I wait. And wait. Most of the other kids have been picked up.

Miss Carter waits with me and three other kids.

"Was your dad working in the city today?" she asks me.

I nod. It's starting to get dark.

"One of the other parents told me the freeway collapsed," Miss Carter says. "Your dad might not be able to get here."

I can't help it. I start to cry. I think I've been holding it in since the earthquake. Miss Carter puts her arm around me. She was always my favorite teacher. I'm actually pretty good at gym.

The police come by at last. They ask if we need medical assistance. We don't.

"A lot of homes are badly damaged," one of them says. "But it's much worse in the city."

My heart seems to stop. Dad was in the city.

The police tell us there are emergency tents in the park. We should go there if we can't go home.

Just as the police leave, three more parents arrive to collect their kids. Now it's just me and Miss Carter.

"We can wait a while longer," she says. "If your dad doesn't come, you can come home with me. We'll figure something out."

It's night now. Even though it's summer, it's a bit cold. I ate my fruit bar hours ago. I'm hungry. And I'm scared. What will I do if Dad never shows up? What if he's dead?

Just then someone appears at the other end of the field. It's hard to see them in the dark. They shine a flashlight at us.

"Amy!" a girl's voice yells. "Amy!"

"Do you know that person?" Miss Carter asks. She shines her phone light back.

As the girl gets closer I see who it is. I do know her!

It's Mara! My half sister!

She starts to run. I stand up just as she reaches us.

Then she throws her arms around me and holds me tight.

Chapter Three

Mara lies. She tells Miss Carter that she's eighteen. Miss Carter believes her. I think she wants it to be true. She wants to get home too. Like I do. Like everyone does.

"Can you walk?" Mara asks. "Are you hurt?"

"I'm fine," I say. "I can walk."

We say goodbye to Miss Carter. Mara leads us back across the field. Her flashlight shows the way. All the streetlights are out. I guess the power is off everywhere.

"Where are we going?" I ask.

"We can't go back to my place," Mara says. "It fell halfway down the hill."

"Is your mom okay?" I ask.

Mara walks in silence. The flashlight beam waves on the cracked road.

"I don't know," she says finally. "She was in the city today. I tried phoning her. I guess none of the networks are running. What about your mom?"

"She's in Japan," I say. "She was going to come home tomorrow. But..."

"All the flights will be canceled," Mara says. "Did you try calling her?"

"Yes, but...nothing," I say.

Mara tells me what she did after the earthquake. She wasn't even at school when it happened. They had a half day today.

"I was at home when everything started shaking. I ran outside just in time to see the house slide down."

I've only seen Mara's house once. I was with my dad when he dropped something off for her. It's a small cottage in the backyard of a bigger house. The yard backs onto a ravine.

"It kind of tipped over," Mara says. "Into the ravine. I couldn't even grab anything. I found this flashlight in the shed."

We continue to walk in the dark. We don't talk for a long minute.

"All my stuff is gone," Mara says. "All my mom's stuff."

I take her hand and squeeze it. She squeezes back.

"I hope the cats are okay," Mara says. "They were outside."

"They'll be fine," I say. I don't know why. I have no reason to think that. It seems Mara wants to hear it though.

"Probably harassing wildlife as we speak," Mara says.

"Poor squirrels," I say.

We both laugh and it feels good. The dark seems a little less scary.

Mara turns us onto the main road. "Your house is up this way, right?" she asks.

"Yes."

My house. I wonder how badly damaged it is. It's not on a hill at least. But it's older. And part of it is under construction. My dad was redoing the kitchen. So it's kind of a mess to begin with. At least we don't have any pets.

We get the answer soon enough. After a few minutes on the main road, we turn onto my street. Some of my neighbors are sitting on their lawns. They are wrapped in blankets. Their faces look haunted.

"Is everyone okay?" I ask my old-lady neighbor, Mrs. Blum. She lives on the corner. She's sitting in a lawn chair with her little dog on her lap.

"I don't know, Amy," she says. "No one was badly injured on this street. But my roof collapsed. And I still haven't heard from my son."

"The phones are down," Mara says.

I know I should introduce her. But I'm still in a daze. I just want to get to my house.

When we're finally standing on my front lawn, I let out a breath. My house looks normal. Dark but normal. Then Mara shines her flashlight up.

All the windows are cracked and broken. Part of the front porch has fallen down. As we get closer we see water seeping from under the front door. Mara breaks some glass out of the window. We peer inside.

The living room ceiling is now on the floor. So are the bookcases. And the TV. There are wires hanging everywhere.

"That doesn't look safe," Mara says.

"What should we do?" I can feel myself starting to cry again. I was hoping Dad would be here. I think Mara was hoping that too. But he's not.

I look around. My mom's minivan is parked in front of the house.

"We can get in there," I say. It's pretty cold now.

Mom usually leaves the van unlocked. She says there's nothing in it worth stealing. And she would rather thieves not break the windows. Sure enough, when we try the door, it is unlocked.

Mara and I climb in. I find a picnic blanket bunched up in the back. And the box of granola bars Mom keeps to give to the homeless.

"We have an earthquake kit," I say. "But it's in the garage."

"We can look for it when it's light out," Mara says.

Once we get comfortable inside the van, I let the tears come. Mara puts her arms around me.

"It'll be okay, sis," she says. She has never called me sis before. Honestly, we've hardly ever spoken. I thought she hated me. I thought she blamed me for our dad leaving her mom. That's how I would feel.

Maybe none of that matters anymore.

"At least we're together," Mara says. "We've got each other."

I wipe my eyes on my sleeve. "Thank you for coming for me," I say.

"Anytime," Mara says.

Chapter Four

We both sleep. It's daylight when someone taps on the minivan window. It's another neighbor, Mr. Fields.

"I'm barbecuing," he says. "Everything in my freezer. Don't want to waste it. Do you guys want a sausage?"

We eat well. A sausage each with slightly scorched hot-dog buns. And hot tea. The mood on my street is almost cheerful. People are picking through their houses. They compare notes.

"My bathtub cracked," one woman says.

"I found my dog!" someone else cries. "He's fine!"

We all cheer. Mr. Fields gives the dog a sausage.

Mara and I decide to check my house. Mara goes first. We carefully step around wires and debris. Mara finds the water is coming from the cracked toilet. It's still leaking. She turns off the water supply.

Dad's half-renovated kitchen is destroyed. The roof has caved in. We manage to salvage a few cans of soup. Some crackers. A bag of oranges. We also get the earthquake kit. It has a water bottle and energy bars. Another flashlight. Emergency blankets. Mara and I divide it all into two backpacks.

I grab some clothes from my room. There's broken glass everywhere. Part of the ceiling and wall has crumbled down.

"It's not safe to stay in here," Mara says.

So we pack up my clothes and go back outside.

The mood on my street has settled. People are sitting on their lawns again. Everyone looks shell-shocked.

"What should we do?" I ask. "Wait for my dad?"

"He's my dad too," Mara reminds me.

"I know. I'm sorry."

Mara pats my shoulder. "It's okay," she says.

"Dad would be here by now if he was coming," I say. "Wouldn't he?"

"If he walked?" Mara asks. "The freeway collapsed, I heard."

"I heard that too. How long would it take to walk?"

Mara thinks for a second. "Maybe twelve hours? A bit longer?"

It's been way more than twelve hours since the earthquake. It's been almost twenty-four hours.

"What if he's hurt?" I ask. I don't say the other thing I'm thinking. *What if he's dead?*

"My mom was in the city too," Mara says. "I left a note for her on the main house." She sighs. "But she would be here too by now."

"Who would know?" I ask. "How can we find out who is injured?"

"I don't know," Mara says. "I saw some police when I was walking to your school. But they were busy with injuries and other stuff."

"I saw some police too," I say. "They told me to go to the emergency camp in the park. Maybe we could try there."

So that's what we do. We each take a backpack full of supplies. And we head to the park.

As we walk, we see some awful things. One of the small bridges over the river has collapsed. There are cars in the water. I don't know if people drowned. An ambulance is helping a woman with her two kids. They are all covered in blood.

Mara takes my hand.

When we arrive at the park, it's packed. Hundreds of people stand in lines. They're noisy. Angry. There doesn't seem to be any police. And I can't tell who is organizing everything. People are yelling. Others are pushing into the lineups. They are waiting for food. For water. For blankets. Mara and I already have these things.

"What's in those backpacks?" a man at the end of the line says. He doesn't look friendly. Mara turns us away. "Hey, girls," the man calls after us. "Aren't you going to share?"

"Walk calmly," Mara says.

I do what she says. When we're a block away, I glance back. The man isn't following us. He's back in line for food.

"That didn't look good," I say.

"No," Mara says.

"I feel like we wouldn't be safe there."

Mara looks to the west. We can just see the mountains north of the city.

"What if we go look for them?" I ask. "Dad and your mom? Maybe they are in hospitals in the city."

"It's a long walk," Mara says.

I glance back at the park, now far behind us. "I think I'd feel safer if we kept moving," I say. "Also we might find somewhere safer to stay. Better than that camp."

Camp, I think. *Refugee camp.* I've seen refugees and displaced people on TV. I never thought I'd be one.

"You're right," Mara says. "Let's go find… something."

Something, I think. We don't even know what to look for. Because we don't know what's left.

Chapter Five

We walk for about an hour. Then it starts to rain. It rains all the time around here. I should be used to it. But it makes me angry. Don't we have enough problems? Why can't God give us a break? Another hour passes and we're soaking wet.

Mara turns us down toward the river. There's a kind of junk depot there. Nobody is around and the offices are all locked. But there's a rusty shipping container on the riverbank. It's open.

Mara and I clamber inside. It feels good to get out of the rain. We eat an orange each. Mara refills our water bottle from the rainwater dripping off the shipping container. She drops a little tablet into it to purify the water.

"We have to wait thirty minutes before we can drink this," Mara says. "I'm going to take a nap. Can you keep watch?"

"Yes," I say. In seconds, it seems, Mara is asleep.

I sit next to her. I watch the rain. The ground outside turns to mud. But we're fairly dry in here. I pull out one of the silver emergency blankets. It looks like something from Star Trek. Spreading it over Mara's body and my legs, I lean back.

I wonder what time it is. My phone battery died hours ago, and I don't have a watch. The rain clouds make it seem gloomy. Is it nearly night? I'm pretty tired. My eyes feel heavy. I'll just close them for a second.

When I open my eyes, it's pitch dark. And the world is shaking again!

"Amy!" Mara yells from somewhere. "Amy, grab your stuff and get out!"

I jump to my feet. I have to feel my way around. Where's the door to the shipping container? Why is the ground shaking again?

"It's an aftershock!" Mara says. "A big one! Get out!"

I stumble toward the sound of her voice. Suddenly strong hands grab me. They drag me out into the mud.

"Run!" Mara shouts. "The bank is about to collapse!"

She drags me up the muddy hill. As we reach the road, the shaking finally stops. I can barely see anything. Mara digs in her backpack. She pulls out a flare and twists it. It bursts to life. Bright as a tiny sun.

Mara holds the flare up. The light shines down the hill. It's just bright enough for us to see the riverbank dissolve in the rushing water. The river swallows the shipping container. The one we were just in.

My legs feel wobbly. My heart is pounding.

It seems like there is nowhere left on earth that is safe.

"Are you okay?" Mara asks, holding the flare over me. "Where's your pack?"

My mouth is dry as I answer, "I left it in the container. It's in the river."

"What?!" Mara shouts. "You had one of the flashlights! You had the food! You were supposed to stay awake!"

"I…know. I must have—"

"You should have kept your backpack on!" Mara is really angry. The red flare lights up her face.

"I'm sorry. I didn't know th—"

"We can't eat sorry!" Mara yells.

I realize it's still raining. The raindrops

hiss on the glowing flare. I'm glad of the rain. It will hide the fact that I'm crying.

"We can look for more food," I say, trying not to sob.

"Where?" Mara asks.

"Let's start here," I say. And I slosh back through the mud to the junkyard office. I pick up a piece of bent pipe on my way. When I get there I put one arm over my eyes. Then I smash the lock on the office door.

I expect an alarm to go off. But nothing happens.

Mara comes up behind me. She leaves the flare on an old car. Digging in her backpack again, she pulls out her flashlight.

We search the office in silence. Stuff has tumbled everywhere. But there's a fridge with some cans of Coke. There's a box of cookies. Some chocolate. We take it all.

I know we're looting. And I know it's illegal. I've heard that in news reports too, about riots and stuff. I never thought I'd be a looter either. But the earthquake changed everything.

Especially me.

Chapter Six

It finally stops raining. The moon comes out. That makes it easier to see where we're going. We walk along the highway for a while. It's cracked in places. But there are still cars trying to get through. The ones that pass us slow down sometimes. People call out to us. Men.

Mara doesn't trust them. We decide to walk along the railway track instead. The moon is bright now. We can save the flashlight battery.

"What time is it?" I ask. The first words I've said in hours.

Mara looks at her watch. "About three a.m.," she says. "The sun will come up soon."

"How far away are we?" I ask. I don't know if I mean "How far away from home?" or "How far away from where we're heading?"

"Far," Mara says. "We haven't even gotten to Maple Ridge yet."

My eyes are drooping again. Soon I feel like I'm sleepwalking. But Mara was right. After another hour the sky starts to lighten.

I look behind us. East. A sliver of light peeks over the horizon. Dawn.

The day brightens. We see destruction everywhere. The railway is buckled. Someone's shed is flattened. A bunch of utility poles have fallen over like toys. Broken power lines lie across the road. They're not sparking. Mara says the electricity must be off. But we're careful around them anyway.

When the sun is fully up, we come around a curve. There's a clearing in the trees. We can see up to the road and beyond. A large group of people is gathered around an old church.

As Mara and I get closer, we see it's not a church anymore. A sign says it's a Sikh temple. There are men in colorful turbans and women in bright cotton tunics. One of the women runs toward us. She looks a bit older than Mara. Maybe a college student.

"Oh my goodness!" she says. "Where did you come from?"

Mara tells her a bit of what we've been through. The woman shouts at someone in another language. Two little boys run up with clean blankets.

Soon we are sitting under a canopy. Other people are sitting with us. White people, Asian people, people in hijabs or saris. The lady who greeted us gives us some veggie curry. She says her name is Amita.

"That's kind of like my name," I say. "I'm Amy."

"Welcome, Amy," she says with a smile. "Please eat. I'm sorry the curry is cold. We ran out of fuel last night."

Amita sighs and looks up at the church/temple. The stained-glass windows are all broken. Her smile falters.

"There are toilets inside if you need them," Amita says. "They still sort of work."

Mara and I look at each other. We've been peeing in the bushes. But I don't want to tell Amita that.

"We're fine," Mara says. "Thank you."

After we eat, Mara suggests I take a nap.

She says, "We're a couple of hours from Maple Ridge. If we start again at noon, we could make it to Burnaby by nightfall. Then walk into Vancouver in the morning."

This gathering is a lot more peaceful than the one in the park. A lot more organized. And everyone is well fed. With Mara nearby I feel safe enough to close my eyes.

I fall asleep instantly.

I wake up to shouting.

Mara is shaking me.

"I think we have to go," she says.

As I sit up and look around, I see soldiers. And my first thought is, "Yes! We're being rescued!"

But kids are crying. Some of the soldiers are waving guns around.

Amita runs toward us. Her smile is gone.

"They are taking children inland," Amita says. "Children whose parents are missing. There is an emergency center in Kelowna."

I look over at the large army truck on the road. Kids are getting on board. But they are crying.

"It looks like some of them don't want to go," I say.

Mara takes my arm. She's tense. Like she wants to run away.

"The kids are scared," Amita says. "But we can't keep them here. Not without their parents. I don't want trouble from these soldiers."

Someone calls Amita's name. She runs off. Mara and I look at each other.

"We could pretend we're older," I say.

Suddenly one of the soldiers starts yelling at Amita and another woman.

"How old are you?" the soldier yells. "I heard there were two teenagers here! Where are your parents? You need to get on the truck."

"Wait!" I say. "We're the teenagers!"

Mara glares at me. But Amita is scared of the soldiers. If she doesn't want to go with them, I don't blame her. She helped us. We can help her back.

"Let's get on the truck, Mara," I say.

I know Mara wants to argue. But she follows me onto the truck.

Chapter Seven

"Great," Mara says. "Now we're going in the wrong direction."

"I didn't trust the soldiers," I say. "Not with Amita and her friends."

"So you thought that *we* should just go with them?" Mara says. "Brilliant." She rolls her eyes.

I put the backpack on. The other kids on the truck stare at me. There are twelve of us here. I'd like to ask them all what happened. If they know where their parents are. Are their parents dead? But of course I won't. I wouldn't want to be asked that.

The truck bounces over the cracked road. All of us kids try to hold on to the seat. A few minutes after we leave Amita, the truck stops. One of the soldiers hands out juice boxes.

Then the ground rumbles. The truck shakes. Some of the kids start to cry. The soldier drops the juice boxes and runs toward the front of the truck.

Another aftershock!

This one is not as bad as the last one. But it distracts the soldiers.

I make a quick decision. I grab two juice boxes with one hand. With the other hand I grab Mara and drag her off the truck. We run back down through the trees.

I stop us when we reach the railway track.

Mara bends over, catching her breath. She laughs. "That was crazy!"

I give her one of the juice boxes. "You were right. We were going in the wrong direction. And I don't trust those soldiers."

We drink our juice as we walk west along the train tracks. We have to step over bent or broken tracks in some places. But apart from that it's okay. Fun even. It's like I'm out for a walk with my sister. We crack jokes. We laugh until we have to wipe our eyes.

There was a lot of sugar in that juice.

At one point the tracks lead us close to the river's edge again. We watch the water for a while. Bits of wreckage float by. Logs. Parts of buildings. A half-sunk canoe.

"My stepdad had a boat he used to bring up here," Mara says.

Her stepdad. I forgot about him. He died two years ago. We never met.

"I'm sorry about...you know," I say.

Mara shrugs. "Thanks. He was a good guy. A good dad. I miss him."

I hear what she's not saying. That her real dad is *not* a good guy. *My* dad. Now I'm feeling sad. About my dad. About Mara's stepdad. About everything.

I wish I'd known Mara when we were little. She's my sister! Why did Dad keep us apart?

I guess the sugary juice has worn off.

After walking for an hour, we reach a train station. Part of the platform has collapsed onto the tracks. All the glass in the entrance building is smashed. But the concrete stairs up from the tracks seem okay. Mara and I climb them. We're careful not to step on glass.

When we get up to street level, we stop. Mara makes a choking noise.

There's an old building there. Or there was. It's completely destroyed. Collapsed.

"Oh no," Mara says.

Police cars and ambulances are lined up along the road. People are looking through the rubble, but everything is silent. I take a step forward. We could help dig. Or something. But Mara takes my arm. She pulls me back.

I yank away and take another step. But then I see them.

Shapes under white sheets. Shapes laid out on the road in front of the ruins.

Bodies.

Mara takes my arm again. But gently this time.

"We should keep going," she says. "We'll only be in the way."

I let her drag me until the ruined building is far behind us.

"We could have helped," I say.

"No one wants a fourteen-year-old's help," she replies.

"I'm fifteen!" I yell. "Almost sixteen!"

"I didn't want you to see," Mara says. "You don't need to see that."

"You think I don't know what's going on here?" I practically scream. "Thousands of people are dead. Possibly…probably our…"

I stop walking. I put my hands over my face. A second later I feel Mara put her arms around me.

"Don't say it," she says. "It will only make things worse."

She knows what I'm thinking. Dad worked in an old building downtown.

"We have to keep moving," Mara says. "That's all. Just keep moving."

She's right. If I stop moving, I think I might go crazy.

Chapter Eight

We reach the Pitt River just before dark. Mara's plan was to cross over into Coquitlam, then walk in the dark as long as we could. Maybe make it to Burnaby.

But we can't cross the river. The road bridge is in pieces. Metal and concrete hang from snapped cables. It just...fell apart. There were probably cars on it when it happened.

I don't like to think about that.

"We could try the rail bridge," I say.

"It's so dangerous," Mara says. "The bridge I crossed to get to you was…sketchy."

"Maybe we should wait for daylight," I say. "So at least we can see any damage."

Mara doesn't even answer. She just throws the backpack down on a clear patch in the bushes.

I try to get comfortable on the ground. Mara goes down to the river and comes back with a full water bottle. I dig out one of the water-purifier tablets. Thank goodness we didn't lose them.

"I've got matches," Mara says. "I could try to make a fire."

"Isn't that…illegal?" I ask. I know some kids

at my school got in trouble for it one time.

"Who is going to stop us?" Mara says. "Also it's cold."

A few minutes later we have a good blaze. I warm my fingers and aching, blistered toes.

"There's a Walmart just on the other side of the river," Mara says. "We could look for a portable phone charger."

"Do you have money?" I ask.

She makes a face. "I wasn't thinking of buying it."

"Right," I say. My face is hot. And not just from the fire. I forgot, we're thieves now.

We sit in silence. The firelight makes everything glow orange.

"Have you ever been camping?" Mara asks.

"No," I say. "Have you?"

I see her nod. "My stepdad liked it. He liked all that stuff. Boating, fishing, camping. We weren't rich. But he used to call nature his castle."

That makes me think of my dad. Always working. Never time to take holidays. He never seemed to think we had enough. He complained that Mom's job should pay more. He thought my grades needed to be better.

Nothing was ever enough for him.

Now it's all gone.

I close my eyes, thinking of that.

When Mara shakes me awake, it's dawn.

"Don't freak out," she says.

"I'm too tired to freak out," I answer. "What's going on?"

"I went down to look at the rail bridge," Mara says. "It's one of those bridges that open for boats to get through."

"Ugh. And it's open?"

Mara nods. "Maybe ten feet? It must have been opening or closing when the quake hit. But it's too far to jump, I think."

I stand and look down at the river. It's not that wide. And the current doesn't look very strong.

"Could we swim?" I ask.

"That's what I was going to suggest," Mara says. "That's what I thought might freak you out."

"I'm not freaked out," I say. "I'm a good swimmer."

We don't waste time. Mara wraps what food we have left and the flashlight in some old plastic bags we find on the riverbank. She puts that bundle into the backpack. Then she ties it to her ankle with one of her shoelaces.

She uses her other shoelace to tie her shoes around her waist. I do the same.

The river is freezing when we step in. We walk out as far as we can, until the water is too deep.

The current is stronger than I thought. I hope Mara is a good swimmer too.

"Stay together," she says.

"Don't fight the current," I say. "Let it carry us downstream. It doesn't matter where we end up. As long as it's on the other side."

"Right!"

We start to swim. We're about halfway across the river when Mara yelps. I turn, treading water and trying to resist the pull of the current.

"What is it?" I yell.

"The backpack!" Mara screams. "It's caught on something!"

I swim as hard as I can. The current is pulling me away from her. But I fight it. At last I reach out and grab Mara's hand. Her head drops under the water for a second.

"No!" I yell. "Turn over on your back!"

Mara turns, but her legs are being pulled down. I feel along her body. I find the shoelace around her ankle. The backpack is below her.

I submerge, feeling my way down. I yank on the backpack, but it doesn't move. My lungs spasm. I need to take a breath.

Flipping in the water, I wedge a foot against the shoelace and shove as hard as I can. It breaks! Mara starts to slip away. My hand lashes out and grabs her just as I come up for air.

"Mara! Mara!"

She's coughing up water. Disoriented.

"I've got you!" I say. Turning my eyes to the shore, I swim with one arm. I hold on to Mara with the other. It seems to take forever. I'm numb and gasping. But finally I feel the riverbed under my feet. I stand, dragging Mara up with me.

"Can you walk? Are you okay?" I shake her.

When we are knee-deep in muddy water, she bends over. She vomits up river water. I help her to the shore.

We collapse, shivering.

"Amy," Mara says after a minute. "Thanks."

"We're together now," I say. Tears blend with the water dripping from my hair. "No matter what."

"No matter what," Mara says.

Chapter Nine

After walking for an hour, our clothes are nearly dry. We walk west, with the rising sun behind us. The backpack is gone. We have no food. No water. But another hour later it starts to rain. Mara and I stand on the edge of the highway, our mouths open. We let the rain fall onto our tongues.

I feel ancient. Like a prehistoric cave dweller. I might forget how to speak. But the rainwater is the most delicious thing I've ever tasted. I close my eyes and hold my arms out. Maybe the rain will wash this all away.

A honking horn startles me.

A truck loaded with water and food pulls up ahead of us. A rosy-faced lady leans out and yells back, "Are you girls all right? Do you need a ride?"

"We're going to Vancouver!" Mara yells. "To look for our dad."

"The cab's full," the lady says. As we get closer I see four kids in the truck with her. "But you can squeeze in back if you want. Have some water or food. Whatever you need."

I grab Mara and run for the back of the truck. We clamber in. Stepping over cases of water and boxes of food, we find somewhere to sit. There are two boys already sitting there. They look around Mara's age.

"That's our mom driving," one of them says. "We came from Kamloops. A bunch of us in trucks. Cleaned out every store and gas station on the way here. Have something to eat."

We open a box and find packets of chips and jerky. Mara opens a bottle of water.

"Where are you headed?" I ask, through a mouthful of food.

"Wherever we can help," the younger boy says. He looks us both over, frowning. "You look like you've had a rough few days. You can cry if you want to. We don't mind."

Mara starts crying straight away, as though his words gave her permission. I put my arm around her. I think I'm all cried out.

They end up driving us all the way into Vancouver. So many people are camped out along the roads. The boys in the truck hand out food and water. We finally get to a part of Vancouver I recognize, near downtown. When we get out of the truck, the boys shake our hands. Their mom gets out and gives us each a hug.

"Was your dad downtown?" she asks.

"He was. We'll find him," I say. But the more time that passes, the less I believe it.

They leave us at the edge of a large field

full of white tents. People are lined up, and we join them. A few minutes later a woman in a uniform comes out. She looks pale and exhausted.

"Any children in line?" she yells. "Anyone under eighteen with no parents?"

People grumble as Mara and I step forward. We're the only ones.

The tents are full of children. The lady in the uniform turns out to be a nurse. She takes our names. She checks us over.

"I'm going to radio the other shelters and the hospitals with your names. If your parents are there, we'll find them."

We wait. They give us more water and food. They tell us they've run out of clean clothes.

After a few hours a police officer comes to find us. He's an older man in a turban. He says his name is Constable Gill.

"Your father worked in the Clark Building, right?" he says.

Constable Gill has a very serious face. I take Mara's hand because I know what's coming.

"The Clark Building collapsed in the quake," he says. "They are digging for survivors, but...it was a very old building."

I nod. Mara's hand grows ice cold in mine.

"I'm sorry," Constable Gill says. "Do you have any other family?"

"Our moms," I say. "We're half sisters. My mom was in Japan on a business trip. Would she have come back?"

Constable Gill shakes his head. "Airports are closed all the way down to Portland. Tomorrow, they say, they will get some of the phone networks working. You can try to call her."

"My mom was at work," Mara says. "Her office is in an old house in Kitsilano. Not far from here."

"The old wooden houses fared quite well," Constable Gill says. "But most people aren't staying in them. They're camping in the park and at the university. I'll radio down there and see if anyone can find her."

We wait for the rest of the day. But no news comes.

Chapter Ten

We're warm in the tent and we're fed. But I don't sleep. Neither does Mara. I stare into the dark and think about Dad.

Just before dawn Mara nudges me.

"There's one more place we can look," she says. "For my mom."

"Where?" I ask.

"Remember my stepdad's boat? I told you about it?"

"Yeah?"

Mara sits up. I can see her in the dim light. "Mom never sold it after he died. She complained about paying for the moorage every month. But it should still be there. And it's not far. In Richmond, just past the airport."

I sit up. "Will they let us just walk out of here? To go look for her?"

"I don't know," Mara says.

I reach out and take her hand. "We started this journey together," I say. "To look for Dad. To look for your mom. We can't give up now."

As quietly as we can, we wriggle out of the blankets.

"Bathroom," I say to one of the adults watching over us.

We do use the porta-potties they've set up. But we don't go back to our tent.

By the time we get to Granville Street and turn south, the sun is up. A lot of the houses we walk past are badly damaged. But people are in their front yards, handing out food. We get some hot coffee.

Just before we reach the bridge to cross into Richmond, we stop. A man and his wife hold out a phone. The phone cable runs back into their house.

"It works," the man says. "I'm a radio technician. It's a satellite phone. Call anywhere you want."

Mara goes first. She tries her mother, but she can't get through. Then I try my mom's cell phone.

"Hello?" Her voice is frantic. There's static on the line. But it's her. It's my mom!

"Mom! It's me," I croak out.

"Amy! Amy! Oh my God! Thank God!"

I listen to her cry for a minute. Then she tells me her plan.

"I'm in LA. A bunch of us are buying or renting trucks. We're going to fill them with supplies and drive as far north as they'll let us. I'm going to try to get to you. Where are you? Where's Dad?"

"I'm in Vancouver with Mara," I say. "Dad is—I think he might be dead."

Then I'm sobbing so hard Mara has to take the phone. I barely hear what they talk about.

"...if we're not at the marina, we'll be back at the refuge center in town," Mara says. "Don't worry. I'll take care of her."

The man takes the phone back. His wife gives us both a hug. I don't think she speaks any English. But some things don't need words.

An hour later we're walking along the marina in Richmond. Some boats are badly damaged, but lots of them look fine. Mara takes my hand again.

"No matter what we find, we're together," she says.

"Forever," I say.

Just then we hear shouting. A woman jumps off one of the boats and runs up the dock, her hair flying.

"Mara!" she screams. "Mara!"

Mara runs into her mother's arms.

I'm not sure what to do. I just stand there. Finally Mara's mom looks at me.

"Oh my God! Amy?" She opens her arms, and I fall into their hug.

Mara's mom, Ellen, takes us back to the little boat.

"I've been trying to get the engine going," she says. "I was going to boat up the river to look for you."

She makes us some soup in the little galley. While we eat we tell her everything that has happened to us. I tell her my mom is trying to get here from Los Angeles.

"Until she does, I'm your mom, okay?" Ellen says. That makes me feel safer than I've felt in days. I was hungry before, but now I'm suddenly starving. Ellen heats up another can of soup and watches us eat.

"You two rest now. Take the bed," she says. "I'll sleep on the deck tonight. But I'm going to keep trying to get this engine going."

Mara and I strip out of our hoodies. We kick off our shoes and peel off our socks. Then we sit on the bed with our legs stretched out. We compare the blisters on our feet.

Mara lies back. I do the same. The boat rocks gently. Up on the deck, Mara's mother swears at the engine. Mara smiles a little, but it quickly disappears.

"Do you think Dad is dead?" she asks.

We hold hands again. This is what has kept me strong. Kept Mara strong. Having each other's hands to hold.

"I don't know," I say. "I think he might be."

"I'm sorry I never got to know you," Mara says tearfully. "Properly, I mean. I should have fought for that."

"It's not your fault," I say. "I didn't fight either. I should have. But we were just kids."

"Dad should have fought for us too," Mara says.

"For you and your mom, you mean?" I ask. "Like after...everything with my mom? And me?"

"No! No," Mara says, squeezing my hand. "For *us*. For you and me. For us to have a relationship. To be sisters."

"We *are* sisters," I say. And I mean it with all my heart. No matter what happens with Dad, I'm never losing Mara. "Sisters forever," I say.

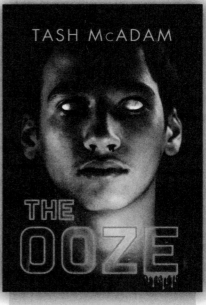

COUNTDOWN
M.J. McIsaac

CAREFUL WHAT YOU WISH FOR
MAHTAB NARSIMHAN

Myles is being blackmailed by someone sending texts threatening to expose a secret that could change his life forever.

Social misfit, Eshana, discovers a website that grants wishes. But is she willing to pay the price to have the life she's always wanted?

ORCA

Gabrielle Prendergast is an award-winning writer, teacher and designer. She has written many books for young people, including the BC Book Prize-winning *Zero Repeat Forever* and the Westchester Award winner *Audacious*. She is also the author of the Faerie Woods series in the Orca Currents line, which includes *The Crosswood*, *The Wherewood* and *The Overwood*. She lives in Vancouver, British Columbia, with her family.

For more information on all the books

in the Orca Anchor line, please visit

orcabook.com